♥

Pocket book

Anneli Sundqvist

©2024 Anneli Sundqvist
Förlag: BoD - Books on Demand, Stockholm, Sverige
Tryck: BoD - Books on Demand, Norderstedt, Tyskland
ISBN: 978-91-8057-853-0

Table of contents

Pocket book

Enter

When we enter,

and when we leave

each other's worlds

let it be with

kindness

Within

Welfare begins
within us.

Two o'clock on Sundays

Tea'...
at two o'clock on Sundays

then, it was time for one cube of sugar
and some drops of milk

it was our tea habits for us
habits we used to share together
and this...little talk...that used to be

between us

at two o'clock I still drink my
afternoon tea'
thinking about it

this time is gone now, but do you still
remember it? at two o'clock, on Sundays.

Am I

The purpose

of your life

is to give your heart

to someone

Am I that someone

Gambling man's hand

Bad cards, on your gambling hand

in life.

it makes you twist and turning

try to do it

find your bad cards throw them away

when you can

get them out of sight from your hand.

try to pick the aces in this pack of cards.

get a better hand

with winning cards.

a gambling man knows if, he has bad cards

it is important to play out the cards right

one by one.

he knows

it can be a winning hand.

The teacher

Let your heart

be your teacher

Thank you

My sunshine, my life.

you

shining so bright

you lightning up my dark

with your light

thank you for your inner

touch

it means so much

without it I wouldn't be much

so always keep in touch

you keep me from fading

or step into an early grave

you save me from ending

my breath

my life complete with you

in it

until my death

...or death do us not apart

is it forever and always

right from the start

in our hearts

Wonder

Wonder

which way to go

take time to wonder

???

before you go

Treasure

Travel in your mind

sit so sometimes

maybe you see

life is inside of you

think of something nice

you have everything

treasure of you

safe inside of you

The rainbow

Have faith,

hope and trust

...that after a rain

it come better days.

I call it, 'to see

the rainbow after the rain'

white dove

Inside
my
heart
lives
a
white dove

I will release it, tonight
I let it fly free
with
a message
to you
of
peace.

so,
let it fly
don't kill it
the symbol
'The white dove'
is
inner peace

when
It reaches you
receive
the white dove
into your heart, into your mind
and
we
will make
peace.

Springs first flower

The branches strongly sway

of the cool but not cold

wind of spring.

and a little squirrel runs

between

the bark covered mighty

trees

on his way home again

while a lot of clouds in the sky

are gathering

and now it feels into the air

soon a spring rain will fall

down

on the ground

and

after that, a sun beam reach,

a

new born flower that looks

up

from the ground.

It starts to live of the light

warm sun.

and this little flower it

become spring first sign of life

when a middle age woman

passing by

she sees springs first sign

of life

Springs first little flower

waking up

from the ground.

Old man's life

A very old man's life...

quiet days

and more quiet nights

wish to live a 'life'

but these days is just an inner

sight from the land of

dreams,

a story. about an old man's

inner life and his dreams

Crossroads

Any way

my way

your way

on our own way

together

or no way

The gardener

This is about
the gardener
this short, and
written poem.

a story of a lovely person
who can handle
the situation to
make a flower
bloom.

the one who knows
how to watering and
fertilize with gentle
means.

someone who
understand a
flowers needs...

with love

Season of spring

I longing for the season
of spring

when everything wakes
within

after the cold winter days
Spring will arrive
with warmer days

it always brings beautiful
memories
in this time of year
'This blooming time'
when all the colours waking
up again
among the flowers a lot of them
with all this love within
everything wakes up
to new life
one more time
once again
the flowers bloom
this is why
I love the spring

Fresh air

Fresh air
is
all around you
like a colourful aura
it
surrounds
you.
with all your
inner
strength
you are a lucky one
with
everything about you
when
all this
aura of happiness
surrounds
you.

Walk like a man

A head
on the top
not everyone has
a head on
without it you can act like a fool
but if you learn from mistakes,
learn from life & follow the policy
and
straighten yourself up in the line
then
with time you learn
to growing up
you learn
to walk like a man

The wind

The wind..

..can change direction

we all know.

all of the time

we all wonder

when & where

will

the wind go

wind is the free power

so, when it's time

put your sail up

if, you learn to sail in the wind

you can decide

when or where

to go

The pearl

mostly

of the time

I'm quiet.

today

I'm looking

on you and

on myself, and this quiet day.

I'm like a mussel,

I am closed into myself

sometimes.

but inside this mussel, maybe you can find

a pearl?!

if, you take a careful look

into my

shell

you maybe find this pearl.

As you are

You are beautiful

Just as you are

So, don't change anything

I love you

just the way

You are

Power

When I take a look ...
into your eyes
I feel so free and come alive
in
the power of your eyes.
your whole existence...
all what you are
it is like a spell
deep
into my heart

but is you true
or do you fool me
when I look into your true? Eyes
and
when we are close
I feel the power

A little spark'

Eyes searching for light

light into another soul,

into another heart.

just something a little spark'

it's all that is needed

so, it come back the light

into these eyes

into this suffering soul.

so, the suffering change to

happiness

into this lonely soul.

Golden rules

A fool always finds his own way

a way no one else want to walk

it takes some time

when he always on the wrong road

you sigh, and think

Oh! What a fool

he is.

but inside this fool

he found his 'golden rules'

from

the road he walked

and that is a big glory

for this fool.

so, maybe he is not a fool

(after all)?!

Solid ground

Love was

that is good history

something that give

some rest in my chest.

peace

all around.

when I put down a foot

I just give it time

and feel?!

that solid ground.

Wisdom

Wisdom, it uses to tell us all

that

all we need is within us.

so, all we need to do is listen

have this inner ear

and with this be able to hear

the

whispers of our inner

wisdom

so, sharpen our ears, this day

and listen

Memories of the past

We cry and dry our tears

we laugh and have some fun,

sometimes.

we live our days

every day we try.

but one day we will part,

that's life

it will be the end of the days

of

'us'

then it all just be a memory

but we keep these memories

the memories of our lived days

into our hearts

or throw them away

we don't care in the past?!

Vivid

You are
a great painter
and
you can handle the brush
like a pro

your day
never
become single black
because
you use every colour
you got
in your palette

you
paint
with style
you make vivid paintings
you make to magic art
there every painting
is like a story, an own tale
to be told.
and you

let them all come alive
On
the cloth.
✧
these
paintings
is
from your brush
filled with
love and passion

it's your love
to paint
it
keeps you alive
on the inside

it's there
the
vivid paintings
born from
...your fantasy

so, now lets
paint
...and let
this inner tale
be told.

Curves

Your smile

can...

make someone else smile.

that little curve

we all need

sometimes

Trust

Trust your feelings

what it tells from inside

you are blind

if you shut your eyes

from what's inside

listen carefully

your path in life

let it be your heart

read the sign

and always be nice and kind

that leads to 'the beautiful' in life

With no words

When you face

a flower, when it bloom

with all the fantasy in this world

there are with no words

that we can tell

a flowers grace,

and sensitive colours

when it bloom

Someday

Some days

I tell you my story

while I go.

someday it's too late

to let you know

so, be careful

with my time

when it's too late

we never know

Just a cloud away

When it comes to the end of this road
you walked together hand in hand
for so long.
then the days will suddenly become
much darker than
yesterday's sunlight.

...it is with no words
we can tell this loss
of a loved one
when
your love
is more
then words ever can tell
and think
if?!
heaven and earth
the distance
between you
is just a cloud away?!
to reach each other
through
'This distance'
is through a thought or...
a prayer?

Every day

Nothing moves
but, the wind

if it not blow my way, today
I do my best anyway

because I know
in the end of the day
I will stand tall, if I do, what
needs to be done,
everyday

The door

Inside my heart

It all breaking apart.

all I see

are your footsteps

leaving me

out through the door

of my heart

The road of life

Step... by step...
I walk a bit of the road
everyday.
I leave some footprints
after me
on this road of life

will I find your footsteps
here beside me
someday.
say, will you take a walk with me
just a little bit
or
all the way
in this lifetime.

sometimes I feel lonely

still

I'm strong

I know

if I find your footprints

here beside me

someday

I will follow them

it can be

you and me

these days

in this life.

so, the question is...

are you ready?

to stand by my side

today!

Respectfully

Not everyone wants to know

or listen to my story

if, then you get to know me

my actions tell if I'm ok

ask your questions

have I answer for them all?

if not... I must discover them more to

know them more

but don't be sure I share them all

with you

respectfully... you know

A curious heart

With
a little curiosity
into our own hearts
we shall live
our day
and
when this curiosity
wakes up
it
makes us start wondering
...maybe make us carefully ask. And
read behind the lines
...try to see behind our own masks
with
this little curiosity
into our own hearts
it
will
give us every day knowledge
so just for us...
...to really listen

The watch

Give & take

Always remember you

Yesterdays

is in the past

but it going to last

inside my memory.

there I have a picture of you

deep in my mind.

I keep it close

so, I will

always

remember

you

Good times

Tell me...

what's the time

if the clock can't say

your heart knows

If its good times

Free me

Free me

from everything

that isn't love

some stay

some go

love

is the only thing

left.

let it stay so

September

Wind blows her hair

in September air

as she walks in silence

thoughts she wears

reflection in her mind

takes her everywhere

even if

she walks nowhere.

Beautiful day

To remember

In this life

don't take life to seriously.

we will all die

but that is another day

so, take your time

all you can

fill it with

happiness,

laughter and a little smile

if you live

your feelings change

all of the time

that's life.

give yourself wings

fly up in the sky

reach heaven above

put your head in a cloud

whatever you do

remember

don't take life to seriously

if the tears will fall

from your eyes

it doesn't mean

you will die

you know it won't last long

this sometimes-childish cry

so, have faith to life

so, a little reminder

don't take life to seriously

because

it isn't the end

of the world

today

just

remember

to

live

this day well

don't let it

just slip away

this beautiful' day

Living

When I sit under the sky
looking up
thinking about God and
his door there up above

Some day we will meet
heavenly father
(you and me)

But, not for a while
but when I sleep can you hold me in
your arms like I am
a little child of god's love.
it would ease my pain
to feel your love
in my sweet dreams
at night

I know my time is not now
it is not time to walk out of life
yet

because
I'm too busy with living

Agenda

To be or not to be
an enemy to myself
what stands on my
agenda?
for the day

All the wars, battles I fight
within myself

all on my own
one by one I take them down

no losers
because
experience I won
in these battles
I fight

all of the time
when I fight myself
the best teacher is myself

so, what will I learn
about myself
when I like to face
myself
today

Nature

Flowers

is better alive

in the green grass

it be found.

let it shine

lovely flowers

of summertime.

pick one you kill it

so, don't.

let it be

your nature of life

Time run

Time run..

faster than we need

will it be time for

the things in life

we need

Sweet blue eyes

It's a
nice
feeling
inside my mind

when the sun
hide
behind the clouds

then
you put your sunglasses off
for a little while
so, then
for a second...
or two
I can see your little smile
and
your sweet blue eyes

when the sun begins to peak
behind the clouds
again
I know
this moment will pass away
quick

but memory
of
your sweet blue eyes
will last
forever

a lifetime

this memory
will be
like a treasure
I keep it close

forever
inside my
mind
memory of
your smile
and
your sweet blue eyes.

Fantasy

In my world
of
fairy tales

my ship is filled
with dreams
I love every one of them
and
in my crew
there are all kind of people
on this sail

every day & night
has its moments

so, take care
of these treasures of dreams
It's there for you at day &night
and
live this day with imagination
and at the end of the day
say goodnight
and
you dream away
when you sail away
to this
another world
...with fairy tales.

The prayer

Do you pray?

down on your knees?

looking for

knowledge?

to stand

up

on your own

two feet

cure me

You cure me
from a lonesome day

with your knock' on my door
...and your sweet hello

you tell me you need me

with an act so polite and
with your tender talk
I feel so fine

you are always
so nice and kind
so, I don't let you go

take a cup of coffee
again
time goes fast
when it's fun
like
today

A piece of heart

Maybe you

give and take

a piece of heart

with someone

you learn to know

along this road

I think

this is

what life is about.

All language

If, it was up to me

I would take your hand

hold you tight treat you right

not like he/she did

he/ she didn't know

what he/she had

if you want see my way

I standing here for you.

this day

you have magic in your eyes

they talk all languages

my heart can see you are a kind one

you magically

Put us through

Love is
what put us through
in this life
we only got some time
because
we only got one life
so, take care of your time
and remember
you not the only one
that need love
in this life
everyone owns a heart
just like yourself
so be nice and kind
to everyone you meet
in this life
don't forget to take your heart
with you...
...were ever you go
and
don't forget to
share a piece of heart?!
with someone
Along the road

Some dear old memories

Some dear old memories
they are so true, to you.
they are your loving pieces of your past
so,
you keep them safe, into your heart

These dear memories
is there to 'stay' inside your mind
while some go..take the high way

you keep them,
some of the memories
that little special one's
you collected them from
a lifetime
close to the heart

you..

..pick them up, someday.
when you start to think, then
they pop up like a surprise, inside
your mind.

when you were thinking that you didn't
remember them

you come to an understand
that some dear old memories
always
stay fresh
when you keep them
deep into your heart
and you know
they will always
be
your
dear memories
from
the past

Be yourself

sometimes
bravery
is to be yourself
it's difficult sometimes
for myself? And maybe someone else?
but this is how we
should live our life
just be yourself
not try to be someone else

if you be yourself
who, you truly are
you can be loved
for who, you really are.
that is true
happiness in life
so, today
just remember
to
be yourself.

Not scared

An echo from the past

come back today

in the shape of a heavy thought

from yesterdays.

but I'm not scared

of anything or anyone, today

so, I turned around

and faced the day

Walking through the room

My eyes...

following your steps

...I see with my heart

and

listen to my head.

'I'm not going to make a move'

I just want to say

give this thought to you

but I can't speak

because

words can't explain

my love for you

I'm out of words

because it is so beautiful

when you

walking

through the room

Puzzle

Like a puzzle
we can resemble
our life

some parts are ok
to share
(with someone you like)

some pieces we
hid in our hearts
until it feels right
to show in the light

and some parts are
completely your own
just for us selves
not to be shown

Footprints

The walk
through life
is like...

...footprints in the sand.

The captain

For real
I'm going down
the ship will sink?
down in the deep dark ground

stop, doing this thing, think so desperate
I say to myself

what's not break you
makes you stronger
in life
just let nothing break you
remember
if, you not love yourself
you will hit the ground
and
that's a failure

so, remember...
...you 'are the captain
on this ship'
so, raise your sail. and sail

The power of a human...

sometimes
we get to know the power of a human
when we are in need then it shows
then
you be my better days
so, just remember to be...yourself.

I need you
by my side every day of my life
so, when you standing there
just remember to be...yourself
because
that's the power of be a human.

you will find out some day
you will come to know 'that day'
when you are in need
a human can be your light n guidance
through those days
these days
you be my power
so, just remember to be...yourself.

Fire

Don't play with fire

just one spark

can put you in trouble

in better or in worse

so, watch up

when you playing

with fire

Love for a lifetime

I took one look into your sweet eyes

in just a second

I had a memory of a lifetime.

in your sweet eyes

I can now find my life, my future

for a lifetime.

all started with this one look

into your eyes

it gave love for a lifetime

Enough

Are you the one

that stay

when my whole world fall

apart

or just when the world leave

will you be there

just be.. you and me

is that enough for you

just be..with me

As long as you are breathing

Something moves in the ashes
a bird looking up, and spread
out the wings, a battle is won
a phoenix from the ground
is rising

new life for this one
this phoenix that is you today?
yesterday it was me
and tomorrow someone else?

the power to live is strong
when it is, a phoenix can be
born.
how many times?
as long as you are breathing

The line

In rain in shine

I walk the line

I hold on

one step at the time

hanging on

take my time give what it takes.

to come home

feels fine

that's why

I walk the line

because

when you around

everything is just fine

On the edge

The fish in the sea
swim so peacefully
but when you take a closer look
you see
to be a fish
is hard to be
and swim in the ocean
isn't what it used to be.
this day's poison in the ocean
come
from human beings
that don't understand
the gift of nature.
so, they destroy the ocean
maybe it's gone it's to late
to save the world
with comfort, selfishness
carelessness
we living on the edge soon.
so, what to do
now.

Nobody cares

When

I'm crying

on my own

who cares

I'm all alone

nobody knows

when the tears are all my own

my darkness

maybe need a light

but my heart is closed

afraid of get to show under

the light

maybe you don't care

this is my fears

so, I keep it

all on my own

I hide my tears.

in the dark shadows

I creep away

from the light

so, nobody knows

so, nobody cares

I'm all alone

Home

The 'switch' is on

the light is on

I'm home

Favourite songs

When time is tough, happy

or sad..

listen to a song

songs are for everyone

but you feel

this one is your own

so, you play it

on and on and on

in repeat all along..

because these ones

is your

favourite songs

True love

If true love
save the soul

I hope love is from you

like I lived today
I will not live the days

hope it better day
tomorrow day

so, let me be loved
by you
my sweet enemy
today, myself.

because true love
can save my soul
everyday

if I just find a way
to love
...myself
today
just like
yesterday
I be ok

Say and do

I feel your love in everything

you say and do.

you so sweet

that's really true

I get by 'thanks' to you

Big man

So

young

and sweet

little one.

still on step one.

with

step by step

trough life

you will be growing up

day by day.

And

be a big man

someday

At night

At night before bed
I meet this horror inside
my head.
in the dark under the light
of the stars
let me rest for a while
through the night.
stronger I am when I feel love
to you, inside of me
and if you love me a little too
that would be
happiness for me
help me through crises in life
with a little love
my power is you
without you horror take a grip
on me
Oh! Lonely me
but I know you right by my side
you are there for me
Oh! Happy me

Your name

My good days

are

you

story of my good days

is

when

your 'name' is written

on my heart

'you'

Open window

The window

is

open

fresh air

breath in, breath out...

feel it?!

the wind and the air

the morning light

is here

a new day to remember

do you feel it

the miracle

of a day

of your life

or does it just

passing by by bye bye..

Carry on

I will walk with you

just take my hand

we take us through

when we are together

we are strong

and we can carry on and on...

if, the road be dark

I will hold you closer

to my heart.

until the end of time

in light in dark

'you'

always there

in my

heart

Out there

on your own

(I thought)

before I get to know

you not so lonely

and not

on your own

not, so lonely

as I thought

No pill

Pain in my head
is made by you
all I need to do
is think of you

no pill helps to fade the pain
because what I need is to erase
you from my brain.
and that is not easy
so, what should I do.
say a finally goodbye
I think that is the best
thing to do

Blessed house

Blessed be this house

House of.
death,
of birth
and life.

Suffer, sadness, anger, sickness
shame, loneliness, guilt, anxious
love, sorrow, helpfulness, tears
healing, helplessness, luck
gossip, hurt, happiness, care
madness, craziness...

house of. questions, answers, beliefs...
endings, new beginnings...

house with history

blessed be this house

we all cross paths
someday
In life
(hospital)

Angels

Do
you believe
in the
angels

that
the
angels
With
their healing voices
they can
help us
through
just
with their whisper
to
you

If you do believe
or
not
it's up to you

if
you do
believe

then...
listen up
...when
...the voice of an angel
speak
inside of you
that little whisper
what it says
to you

Fit as one

She felt
she was alone
and she felt she need
to tell someone.
because
she wasn't ready
to face the day and nights
only
by herself

everyday.

so, finally...
one day she found 'the one'
she felt
this was the right one
after her story be told
about her life... And the other side...
she felt peace inside
she finds a good friend
in this one
she was no longer
lonely on her own.

They come to be
best friends
they now felt
they were like two puzzle pieces
fit as one.

When I met death

I met death yesterday

I faced it

in a store, when I was looking
for some snack's

but it was just a play
a Halloween doll
stand in my way.
it was Halloween that day
so, I still alive today
so, lucky me
I die

...another day.

It's a love thing

Love spiritual thing

It makes your heart sing

when you, you, you...

is everything

then I know ..it's a love thing

Meet again

Wish you
where here
maybe
we meet again

someday.

that day
will be
a
happy day

Time

Young heart...
It's time
for
new shoes

Life's math

The math of life

you must do it right

understand it right

if you not have

an answer by yourself

add a friend to your life

a good friend helps you

subtracts problems

in life

Teardrops

My tears
are
everywhere
now.
from my eyes
this
teardrops fall
like a rainy day
it
just pour and pour.

I drown
in my own tears
they falling down
on the ground
and I can't see clear
in this flood of tears

its
heavy days
and heavy nights
without you
this lonely Wednesday

I try to survive
the first day
without you

your voice
wish it could be like before
when your voice felt like home.
but I know
you don't here to love me this way today
because our life together
it ended yesterday

so, I can't
breathe you in
anymore
but I have hope
for you
that love will find you
were ever
you are
make you happy
and stay with you
that my wish
to you

Louder

A world
without words
what a quiet one.

but
silence
will be heard.

sometimes
silence speaks
louder than words.

Guide

Everyone

can be a master

to you

let their inner light

be your guide

today

In the end of the road

When it is...
..In the end of the road
what's the truth
to be told?!
about your days
are you pleased
or do you regret
your steps in life
in the end of the road
there lay some truths
be a wise man in life
read the signs
watch your steps
in time
so, look up
in time
so
you
don't need to regret your life
peace.

Beautiful darkness

This night, tonight

when the lights go out

It's a starlight's night, tonight

you stand in the shadows of darkness

here you find rest for the soul

this night, all these stars shine for you

in...

...a beautiful darkness.

★

Every day

I'm

Thinking

on tomorrows,

thinking on yesterdays,

thinking on todays

I make some thinking

for every day

thinking can make me

understand

I'm just to

wonder

with of the days will make me

understand

sometimes

sometimes
we talk to little
when it would be good
to talk a little bit more
and
sometimes we talk too much
when it would be good
to be more quiet.

To feel good
inside
we must all

have the right skill
to talk and communicate
with
the right
balance.

✧

Lonely heart

At this moment
someone
sit so lonely
even if they have
a person there at their side
cry fill this heart
so quietly inside
every day in this life
they lonely as they can be
why this pain not be seen
together still apart
this is
a lonely heart
for me.

Dearest one

Plz
Hold my hand
out there
in this world
Plz
always be a friend
and
never let me down.

I need you
much these days
so plz
stand by my side
today

you always put
me on the right track
when I'm lost
You
show me the way
home
again

again, and again...

you are and will always be
the dearest one
to me.

and, yes...
you will be
the whole world
to me.

History of our heart's

These memories
every day
with you
are the best days of my life
today it is sweet memories
this days from the past
but it's a safe ground of love
for me to stand on
I'm happy for every day
we made.
I hope you feel the same
of
the time we had you and me
these days
these old days
we
keep them into our hearts
they will last a lifetime
the history of our hearts

Today

I walking
my streets

it's
a walk
on my own, today.

everything I got
is myself,
and my heart, there I carry
all my memories
of the present and the past.

everything I need
are my clothes and myself
and this love
in my heart

so, with this I will carry on, on and on
just must remember to do my living well
live today, because
tomorrow is
..another day.?!

The price

Life is a journey
we all pay a price
to keep us selves alive...
for this trip in life
is it worth the price
you must ask yourself
sometimes

Close to my heart

You exist
into my mind
but I'm afraid that slowly
it will fade away
the years passing by
it is what make the memories
fade away with time
an old photography
help me remember
you
as you were
I save it
close
to my heart

Ocean

You are deep... like the Ocean
and
I love to dive into you.

Tomorrow

When I wake up
tomorrow
then you no longer here
with me.
then I miss you.
but, in the corridors of my heart
there you still wander.
forever
you still with me
inside my heart
I carry you
my little angel
you
are.

But now

Shadows slowly fall

over me

in peace and harmony.

stars and moon above me

dreaming my dreams

in the safe of the night

tomorrow is another day

but now.. I dream.

Great future

Lovely words are spoken,

and it is 'whispers' of a great future

in the air.

great looks, soft lips

sweet skin

beautiful eyes

nice clothes

but for real

it's just for some time

you know

so don't deny it for yourself

this one is

a sweet player.

Power

A flower, what a power

of beauty.

all the

colours and scentses

for everyone.

let us take a glance into

our own hearts

what will we find

when we deal with a flower

I think we all feel it's power

when we face this flower.

Nightmares

I try to sleep..

with my head heavy like a

stone

on the pillow case.

I try to sleep until tomorrow.

happies time is in my dreams

there a nightmare 'is' only

'a dream'

when I wake up

everything else is real

then, it's a nightmare

for

'REAL'

Aces

Maybe..

I don't know of many people

as my friends.

but I comfort myself

I got the best cards

I only got the aces

and I hold them

close

to my heart

I am

I am..

Like a tear in your eye

I am..

Like a stone in your heart

I am..

Like the gravel in your shoe

And..

I am still wondering

What makes you still love me.

Great healer

Pain is inside my chest
like a wounded one
I am
I try to escape
but I can't run away
from this shot
In my heart.

I am like the target
with
the bullet right into my heart

Now, I need to heal my heart
put the pieces right
back to the right place
try to get it back
there it was
from the start

I can heal..
with the soft words of love
in my ear
I hear these words
in a speak or a song

I play for myself

It heals my pain
with those words
and
these songs..

words are so strong
so, it fades my scar away
this way
day by day

we will see
if I live
tomorrow
love
is not a game
its 'live or die'
on the inside

love
it gives and take
and real love is
a great healer
I say.

this words
of love..

can help you
to carry on
on and on...

September air

I come walking down the street

with the wind in the hair

in this cold September air

I felt happiness

inside

when I was walking down the line.

with you in my mind

so true.

I walking with my thoughts

of

'you'

Gone fishing

Grab it

hold on

don't let go

just a little bit more

you done it

fishing

about something

you need to know

now the answer

is on the fishing line

so, do your best

to drag it

into dry land

Strong coffee

I went on a funeral

in the season of spring

it was a good friend of mine

it was time to put him in

to his final sleep

in a light brown coffin, he finds his rest,

with white and pink flowers

put on his chest.

When it was my time to say

that final goodbye

I had tears rolling down

from my eyes.

after the heartfelt ceremony

we take a drink

It was the darkest strong coffee

I have ever tasted

In my life.

a memory

like this

will stay for a lifetime

so, my dear friend

at last...

may you rest in peace.

R.I.P

In tomorrows

If

I'm

Out of love

and

It feels like love is gone

then, I put my trust

in tomorrows.

so, the word

'HOPE'

is the word

for

tomorrows

My fuel

I love coffee

when I need it

Coffee will be my gasoline.

when I need it ?

I say

every day.

how should I otherwise

live the day.

Words of love

I'm a little frozen

so, why do you not speak

with me

I need to listen

to your voice

it always keeps me warm

when I hear you speak

The words of love

Navigate

Just stormy waves?
on your sea.
you must understand
"no one can control the weather"
only thing we can do
is handle the sail
sometimes, we must put
down
the sail
let the storm pass
after that we can raise our sail
again.
so, we must all read the weather.
and learn to navigate
on the compass rose
it will help and tell the way
we must all learn to navigate
in different stages
of life
if you do
your ship will
sail safely through.

Let it be spoken

When the words of love

at last

be spoken

then it can heal

broken souls and broken hearted

in this world

of craziness

and darkness

let love be

the guide

for you

let love be the light

for you

and erase the darkness.

The same

I wander through life

night and day

explore my world

inside my shell

I find you there in

my thoughts and mind

every time of the day

in my heartbeat to myself

I say thanks'

for your time

all in my heart

I protect it well

You do the same

Truth

True?

are you?

really?

liar?

you are a big talker?

or quiet?

tell me about it

who are you

can I believe in you

so, do you tell me the truth

Or

are you just

a liar

What a gift

You

are my everything

love is like a magic between us

I'm blessed by you and you by me

something to looking forward to

every day with your love

day by day

I say thanks for everything

you give.

when I'm with you

I have everything

what a gift

The power of love

The power of love
is something
that start deep inside
and
in a heart filled with love
there exist
possibilities
for everyone.

just to remember
it maybe takes some time
to handle love inside
but, give it time
let it grow
then
we will see a heart in full bloom
within
soon.
do you feel
such a beautiful sight
✿
a blooming heart
can be
for everyone.

153

On the line

I'm curious
if I fish, I will see what fish there are
in this sea.
just waiting for that 'special one'
so, my curiosity is on, the fishing line.
with a proper fishing technique
I will catch
the right one.

Own truths

Windows,

mirrors,

neighbours, people..

they all tell who you are

in their own different ways

but, what's the truth when

everyone has their own

truths

Blues

Beautiful songs...
...can be born
from a broken soul
so, don't say
bad days ain't wort nothing at all

When time is tough
listen to these words
in these written songs.
when life give you
sad eyes and a sad heart
what you got is the death
for your soul
if, you close your heart.

poor is the closed hearted, within
rich are love
this is human nature

the right song
shared
with a sad heart
that's the cure
of
'this blues'

try
to find these songs
then you will find
peace
deep in your heart
when you feel
you are not
alone

'Now'

Cold wind of death
will
'come'
one day.
with that last peace
for you
or
someone else.
this is the true rule.
everyone alive
in this life
no one of us
can run away
even if you try
your best
to escape and stay alive
this way
you
someday
try to win some time
with
hide and seek
you hide
death seeks

but it won't do
because
wind of death
will simply find you
everywhere
whatever you do.
the wind of death
will
take you away
of here
that's 'the end' of you
then
peace over you
but before that
remember
to live to your last breath
'stay alive'
live this life
'now'.

Try again

Love was a fire
and now it has become aches
but a phoenix will rise again,
maybe already tonight
if, you feel ready

the time is in

so, just spread your wings
and fly
again

this fire
of love
burn into
your soul
like a fire

just you dare

to try
again

Listen

I do not believe

in what you say

because you think

you know everything all by

yourself

if, you listen

what I say

you hear someone else than

yourself

The tale

The ink bleeds

like blood from my pen

I try to create

words that give

a meaning in life.

with all these letters

I can tell a tale

if, I just find the right words

so, maybe

I can show you, and open up

a whole new world

Life

Someone writes on

their first

sentence.

while other

conclude on the

last verse

Not a wasted day

It takes another day and night

before another day is born

just like yesterday

but you need to know

take care of this day

so, what you got is

a memory of a beautiful time

not just a wasted day

If

If, you are lost,

looking for a shore

..or arms to hold you close.

"I'm here for you" God always told

from your youth, to the day

you fall down into your grave.

in his arms he hold you warm

he hears your deepest pray

when you call god's name

when you give all, you got, and put the

words right

then, you

looking for a sign

so, maybe someday,

you will find your sign

The language

Language of love

can you spell

to

l.o.v.e ?

sometimes it feels

we got so, much

to learn.

One single tattoo

One, single blue tattoo

you put it on,
on the best place
of your arm

Tattoo's
got a lot
of
stories to tell

Only got
one single tattoo?

it's
only one tattoo
yes,
but I say..

...it will stay there

for a
lifetime

A Dodge

Home is a place
that always be your
special place.

something
to longing for
when you are out on the road

you feel
this dearest place
always be close
when, you keep it
deep in your heart

when you pull the gas
and drive away
with your Mercedes, Dodge..
or what you got

just remember
you are always welcome home
to that little place
you call your own
H.O.M.E

Fish on the shore

I lived fully alive

the blood in my veins was

pumping around

to swim in the ocean

made my days.

I found a beautiful heart

and fell for this love.

now

that is just memories

of yesterdays

inside my now broken heart.

now

I feel dead like a fish

that laying on the shore

flat on the back feeling

I can't live anymore.

I get my heart crushed and I think

I'm dead for sure this time

it feels like I am living on the edge

when you took my life from me

when you go

and

you took my heart with you

when you leave, that's for sure.

the worst is you don't care in me

.

anymore.

so let me be dead when I lay

there

on the shore

better be dead than being

alone?!

but

before you leave

give back my loyal and

faithful heart

and don't forget to throw me back

into the ocean

there I was from the start

need the ocean otherwise

I be dead.

we said goodbye but

it didn't need to be

'chop of the head'

I learned in life love is

something

we cant own

love is a gift

so, it is for everyone.

one day you got it and

next day

It's gone.

love is like oxygen it needed

there in the air

you need it to breath it to be

alive

so, try to breathe it if you care

it does exist but will you find

it

out there?!

if you need look

everywhere.

Jealousy

Jealousy in your mind

breaks down the good inside?!

hey! Fight it a while

maybe the bad can be undone

what is it to win? or to lose?

don't shit on the love rule

it just to make a good choice

what's right

you choose.

See you in heaven

The sorrow is sneaking

behind my door

with a message about a loved

one to go.

It's time for this friend to go

climb the stairs

and open the door to heaven.

I don't want to say

that 'goodbye' for ever.

It's to hard to walk

that lonely road forever.

So, I say 'see you in heaven'

I know some day we will meet

again

until then we must believe in it

a way to survive is

to take one step at the time

when sorrow knocked' at my

door

..and sneaking in

only comfort is to believe in it

it exists a

'see you in heaven'

In your head

I see..

you got beautiful eyes
but I still not know
what you got inside

why we not talk
to find out
who? Hide inside.

so, let us chat or chill
for a while?!

show me what you got
inside

Love

L.O.V.E

LOVE BELIEVE IN YOU

Art gallery

A painting

there the paint has faded a little

nevertheless, it is nice

nicest thing

for me

it is made by you

your joy

visible in the colours.

your brush strokes

as a story

there for me

to see

179

180

Thank you!

For reading my book